Emmy
the Exaggerating
Elephant

Fenton
the Fearful Frog

Gertie
the Grungy Goat

Herbie
the Happy
Hamster

Ivy
the Impatient
Iguana

Ollie
the Obedient
Ostrich

Perry
the Polite
Porcupine

Queenie
the Quiet Quail

Rupert
the Resourceful
Rhinoceros

Wendy
the Wise
Woodchuck

Xavier
the X-ploring
Xenops

Yori
the Yucky Yak

Ziggy
the Zippy Zebra

NOTE TO PARENTS

And One More Makes Ten
A story about counting and addition

In this amusing story, Herbie the Happy Hamster needs ten chairs for a party. So, one by one, he borrows a chair from each of his ten neighbors, adding one more chair to the number he has collected until he has a total of ten.

While enjoying this story with your child, you can use it to help reinforce an appreciation of numbers and mathematics. The events in the story can help your child understand the concept of addition and see the relationship between a numeral and the quantity it represents. When you've finished reading the story with your child, you will also enjoy doing the activity at the end of the book together.

For more number fun, let your child count and add more as opportunities present themselves. For instance, count items in the grocery bag when shopping, count plates and forks as you set the table, or count red cars as you drive or ride on the bus.

The AlphaPets™ characters were conceived and created by Ruth Lerner Perle.
Characters interpreted and designed by Deborah Colvin Borgo.
Cover/book design and production by Norton & Company.
Logo design by Deborah Colvin Borgo and Nancy S. Norton.
Grolier Books is a Division of Grolier Enterprises, Inc.   Printed and Manufactured in the United States of America

And One More Makes Ten

RUTH LERNER PERLE

Illustrated by Judy Blankenship

1 EMMY
2 VINNIE
3 FENTON
4 JUSTIN
5 LIZZY
6 DELILAH
7 ALBERT
8 CONNIE
9 GERTIE
10 PERRY

GROLIER
B O O K S

One day, Herbie the Happy Hamster was walking home from the park. Humming a happy tune, he waved to his neighbors as he passed by.

"I'm lucky to be living in such a friendly neighborhood," Herbie thought. "I think I'll have a party and invite all my neighbors," he said to himself.

The next morning, Herbie called everyone who lived in his neighborhood.

"I'm having a party tomorrow afternoon," Herbie said to each one. "Will you come?"

All his neighbors said they'd be glad to come.

"Let's see, how many guests will there be?" Herbie asked himself, counting on his fingers. "Emmy—that's one. Vinnie—that's two. Justin is three. Fenton makes four. Lizzy, five. Delilah, six. Albert, seven. Gertie, eight. Connie, nine. And Perry makes ten."

Later that morning, Herbie went to the AlphaPet Party
Store and bought ten of everything:

Ten pointy
party hats.

Ten red cups.

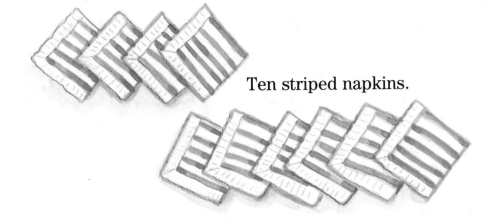

Ten striped napkins.

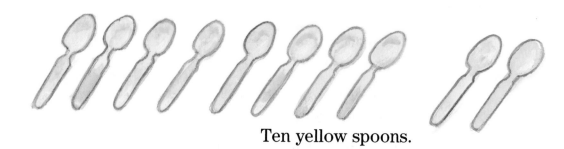

Ten yellow spoons.

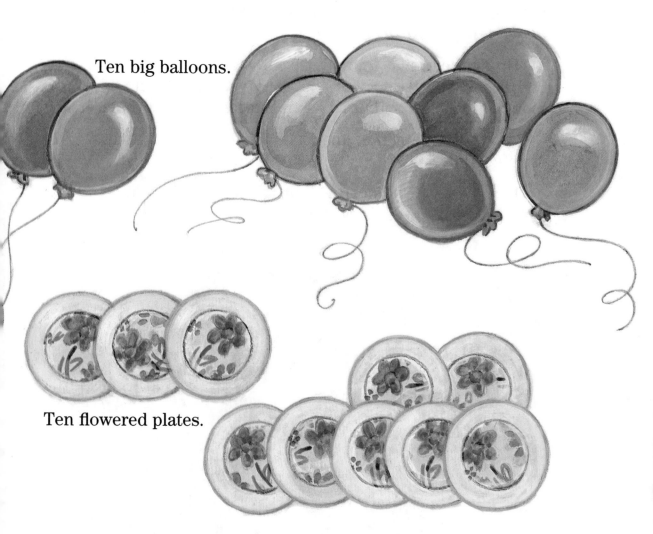

Ten big balloons.

Ten flowered plates.

When he was finished shopping, Herbie picked up his packages and went to buy a cake. Then he hurried home.

When Herbie came home, he started preparing for the party.

"I want everything to be absolutely perfect for tomorrow," he thought.

So Herbie swept the floors, wiped the shelves, and polished the table. But when he dusted the chairs, he noticed they were all scratched.

"Hmm, these chairs could use some fixing up," he said. So Herbie carried the chairs out to the garage. Then he took out his paint and brushes and started to paint them.

It was evening by the time all ten chairs were painted. Herbie left them in the garage to dry, and went to bed.

"I can't wait for tomorrow," he thought to himself. "We'll have the best party ever!"

Early the next morning, Herbie decorated his dining room with balloons. Then he set the table.

"Now all I need are the chairs," he thought. So he went out to the garage to get them.

But when Herbie picked up the first chair, *squish!* His hands got stuck.

"Oh, no!" he cried. "The paint is still wet! Now what will I do? Everybody will be here soon and there's no place for them to sit! Where can I possibly get ten chairs?"

Then Herbie had an idea. "I know! Maybe my good neighbors can help me," he said with a smile.

Herbie made a checklist of all ten of his neighbors.

"Now, if everybody lends me one chair, I'll have just enough," he said.

Herbie hung his checklist on the side of his pickup truck, jumped in, and drove to Emmy the Exaggerating Elephant's house.

When Emmy came to the door, Herbie explained what happened. "Will you lend me a chair for our party?" he asked Emmy.

"Of course!" said Emmy. She ran into her living room and returned with a fancy velvet armchair.

"This is my very biggest and best chair. How absolutely divine to have it at the party," she said.

Herbie thanked Emmy, put the chair on his truck, and checked Emmy's name off his list. "That's one chair," Herbie said.

He waved goodbye and drove to Vinnie the Vocal Vulture's house.

1 EMMY
2 VINNIE
3 FENTON
4 JUSTIN
5 LIZZY
6 DELILAH
7 ALBERT
8 CONNIE
9 GERTIE
10 PERRY

Vinnie was looking out the window as Herbie drove up.

"Hi, Vinnie," Herbie called to him. "I need to borrow a chair. Will you help me?"

"A chair! A chair!" said Vinnie. "It will give me the greatest pleasure to help you. Yes, indeed. That's what neighbors are for! To help each other! Why, I can remember when . . ."

"Vinnie, I'll be glad to listen to your story another time," Herbie interrupted. "But my party is this afternoon. Do you have a chair I can borrow?"

So Vinnie brought a chair to Herbie and helped him load it onto the truck. "Thank you, Vinnie," said Herbie. "Now I have two chairs."

The next stop was Fenton the Fearful Frog's house.

"I need ten chairs for my party," Herbie said. "I already have two. If you lend me one more, I'll have three."

"Well, I guess you can borrow my blue recliner," Fenton said, "but please be careful not to tear it or get it dirty."

Herbie promised to be especially careful and put Fenton's chair on the truck. "Now I have three chairs," he said to himself as he drove off.

It was getting late, so Herbie rushed over to Justin the Joking Jackal's house. When Justin brought out a chair, he slapped Herbie on the back and said, "Looks like you're the *chairman* of the neighborhood, Herbie—get it?" Justin laughed and laughed.

Herbie chuckled as he picked up the chair and added it to the others. "Three chairs plus one more makes four chairs," he said.

Next, Herbie drove across the street to Lizzy the Lazy Lamb's house and asked her if he could borrow a chair for the party.

"You can borrow my rocking chair," she said. "But you'll have to move it yourself. It's too heavy for me."

"No problem!" said Herbie, and he carried Lizzy's chair down the steps and over to his truck. Herbie moved the four chairs together to make room for one more. Then he added Lizzy's chair.

"One, two, three, four, five. Now I have five chairs," he said happily. "That means I need only five more."

Herbie's next stop was Delilah the
Demanding Duck's house. She gave him
a wicker chair.

"Be sure you return it as soon as the
party is over. It's my very favorite chair,
and part of a set," she said. "Handle it
with care, you hear?"

Herbie promised to do everything Delilah asked and
placed her chair next to the other five. "Now I have six
chairs," he said, wiping his forehead.

Albert the Absent-minded Alligator was sitting on his porch when Herbie drove up.

"I saw you collecting chairs, Herbie," he said. "I had a yellow chair all ready for you, but now I don't know where it is."

Herbie smiled. "I know where it is, Albert!" he cried. "You're sitting on it!"

Albert got up and helped Herbie carry the yellow chair to the truck. "Six chairs and my yellow chair make seven chairs," Albert said.

Herbie thanked Albert and drove off.

"Hmm, I wonder why Herbie needs all those chairs?" Albert muttered.

When Herbie arrived at Connie the Cuddly Cat's house, she gave him a big hello and a warm hug. "You can have my favorite seat," she said, and she gave Herbie a soft, furry chair.

"Thanks!" Herbie said. "That makes eight!" He looked at his list. "I need only two more chairs to make ten," he said, driving off.

Herbie picked up another chair at Gertie the Grungy Goat's house. It didn't look much better than his own chairs before he tried to fix them, but at least it wasn't covered with wet paint.

"I guess this chair could use a little fixing up," Gertie said, wiping off the dust with her skirt.

"Never mind," Herbie said. "I'll clean it up a bit as soon as I've collected all the chairs I need."

Herbie counted the chairs on his truck. "One, two, three, four, five, six, seven, eight." Then he loaded Gertie's chair. "There, that makes nine chairs!" he said. "But I still don't have enough."

"How many more will you need?" asked Gertie.

"Just one more," Herbie called as he drove off.

Finally, Herbie reached the last house.

"Good morning, Herbie," called Perry the Polite
Porcupine. "Can I help you?"

"Yes," Herbie said. "I have nine chairs for my party.
Will you lend me one more?"

"Of course. I'll be glad to," Perry said. "If I give you
one more, you'll have ten."

"Ten is all I need," Herbie said with a sigh of relief.
Perry helped Herbie add the last chair to the nine already
on the truck.

"Thank you very much," said Herbie.

"You're quite welcome, I'm sure," said Perry as he
waved goodbye.

Slowly and carefully, Herbie drove back to his house.

He unloaded the chairs and then, one by one, he carried them into his dining room.

"One, two, three, four, five, six, seven, eight, nine, ten," Herbie counted. "Ten chairs for my ten guests."

Soon the AlphaPets arrived at Herbie's house. When they were all seated, Herbie came in with a big, beautiful cake. There were ten lit candles on it—one for each of his ten guests.

Herbie set the cake on the table, and everybody helped blow out the candles. After Herbie served the cake, he went to sit down with his friends.

"Oh, no!" Herbie cried as he looked around the room. "There's no place for me to sit! I need another chair!"

"No problem!" called Justin. "We'll make you the best seat in the house!"

Justin showed the AlphaPets how to make a people-pyramid. Then Herbie climbed over their backs and up to the top.

"Hurray!" Herbie shouted. "I have the best chair of all—a friendship chair!"

Look back at the pages in this book and see if you can find:

1
one cake

2
two spoons

3
three plates

4
four napkins

5
five cups

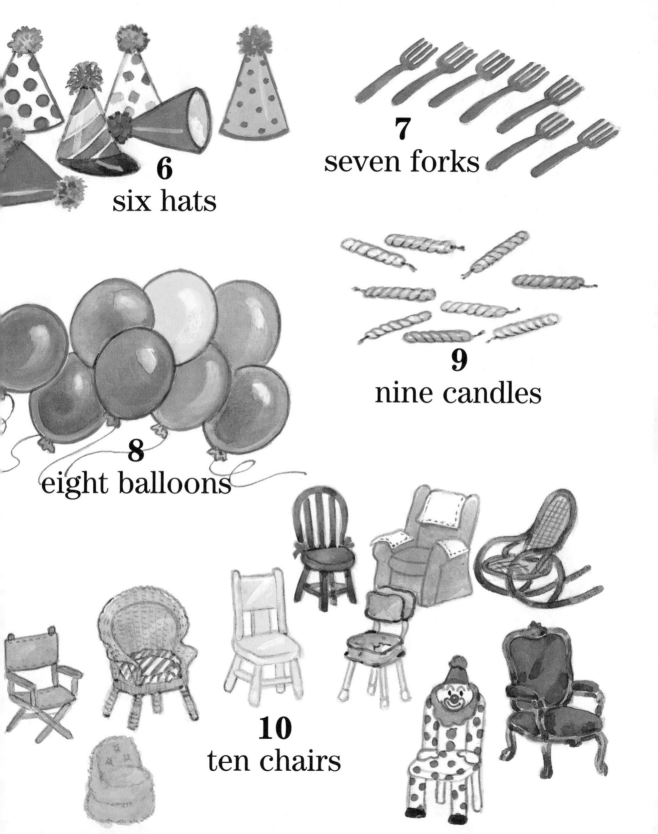

6 six hats

7 seven forks

8 eight balloons

9 nine candles

10 ten chairs

Know Your Alphabet

Aa Bb

Gg Hh

Mm Nn Oo Pp

Uu Vv Ww